For Jack

ORCHARD BOOKS
96 Leonard Street, London EC2A 4XD
Orchard Books Australia
32/45-51 Huntley Street, Alexandria, NSW 2015
First published in Great Britain in 2003
First paperback publication in 2004
ISBN 1 84362 186 X (hardback)
ISBN 1 84362 362 5 (paperback)
Text and illustrations © John Butler 2003
A CIP catalogue record for this book is available from the British Library.
1 2 3 4 5 6 7 8 9 10 (hardback)
3 4 5 6 7 8 9 10 (paperback)
Printed in Singapore

Can You Cuddle Like a Koala?

John Butler

ORCHARD BOOKS

Out in the wild,

what can you be?

Can you copy these creatures?

Are you ready?

Let's see.

Can you **cuddle**
like a koala,
holding on tight?

Can you creep like a mouse

in the pale moonlight?

Can you swing

like a monkey in the tall, swaying trees?

Can you **Wink**
like an owl, hiding
in the leaves?

Can you

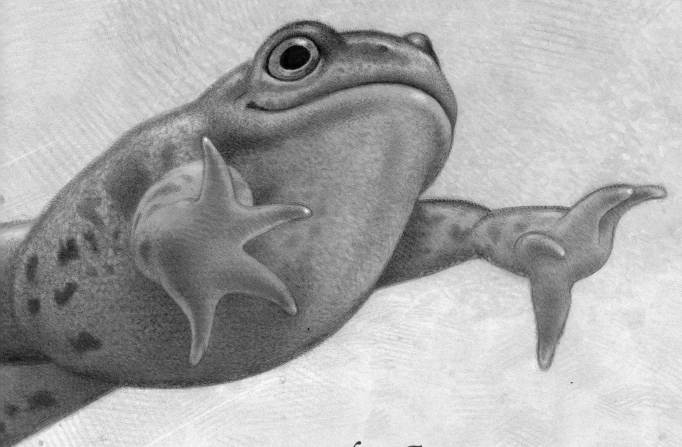

leap like a frog
in the bubbling stream?

Can you s t r e t c h

like a tiger, waking from a dream?

Can you

splash

like an otter

in the pool so blue?

Can you **jump** like a hare,

chasing through the dew?

Can you hug
like a bear,

with all your might?

Can you **curl up** like a squirrel getting ready for the night?

Now look at these creatures, all ready for bed.

Can you copy them too,

and rest your head?